BOO-HOO MOO

By Margie Palatini

Illustrated by Keith Graves

KATHERINE TEGEN BOOKS
An Imprint of HarperCollins *Publishers*

Boo-Hoo Moo

Text copyright © 2009 by Margie Palatini   Illustrations copyright © 2009 by Keith Graves

Manufactured in China.

www.harpercollinschildrens.com

Library of Congress Cataloging-in-Publication Data
Palatini, Margie.
  Boo-hoo moo / by Margie Palatini ; illustrated by Keith Graves. — 1st ed.
    p.   cm.
    Summary: When Hilda Mae Heifer's trademark "moo" starts sounding even worse, the other animals decide she is lonely and hold auditions to find her some singing partners.
    ISBN 978-0-06-114375-5 (trade bdg.) — ISBN 978-0-06-114376-2 (lib. bdg.)
    [1. Cows—Fiction. 2. Domestic animals—Fiction. 3. Animal sounds—Fiction. 4. Humorous stories.] I. Graves, Keith, ill. II. Title.
PZ7.P1755Bl 2008   2007024417
[E]—dc22   CIP
                                                                                                                 AC

Typography by Jeanne L. Hogle
1 2 3 4 5 6 7 8 9 10
❖
First Edition

Next!

Hilda Mae Heifer was down in the dumps.
Feeling low. Sounding like it too.
Even her moo was blue.

OO-OOOOO.
BOO-HOO-MOO."

The goose shook his head.
"Wow. That is one unhappy cow."

"BOO-HOO-MOOOO."

"She sounds miserable," said the hen.
"I second that," said the pig. "That
blubbering bovine is ruining my siestas.
I haven't slept in days!"

Even when *Hilda* was at her happiest, she was far from the best singer. Now these new blue boo-hoo moos were more than everyone's ears and earplugs could take.

But what could they do?

Not much.
Day . . . after day . . . after day . . .

Hilda hung her head and blue
mooed from barn to pasture.
Pasture to barn.

And finally, she would just come
home and stall out.

"MOO-oooo-ooo-o."

"I believe *Hilda* is lonely," said the cat. "I don't think she likes singing solo."

"Mi-mi-MOOOOOooo-Boo-HOO-mooooo!"

The pig covered his ears. "I'm not fond of her singing solo myself."

"She needs help," said the cat.

"I couldn't agree more!" said the pig.

"What Hilda needs is a partner," continued the cat. "I bet a duet would be just the thing to lift her spirits!"

The hen gathered her chickies and clucked. "Why, of course. Two is always better than one! *Especially* if the other can carry a tune."

"Then—why not a trio?"
added the goose.

"A quartet!" chimed in the pig.
"The more the merrier! I know it
will make me happy."

So the four decided to help Hilda Mae lose her Boo-Hoo Blues. They would find the off-key cow some singing partners.

But just who to moo? That was a difficult decision. They made a list:

1. Singers who didn't sing too loudly. ✓
2. Singers who didn't sing too softly. ✓
3. Singers who had talent! ✓ ✓ ✓

"Actually," said the cat, "I think a **Mew mew mew** would sound lovely with a **Moo moo moo**. In fact, I spent a good deal of my youth warbling at the moon. I believe I will sing with Hilda."

"YOU?" cried the surprised threesome.

The goose waddled over to the cat and cleared his throat.

"Uh, just a minute there, fuzz face. If any of us is going to have a sing-along with the cow . . . it's yours truly."

"YOU?"

"My honking is legendary. Get a load of this—

"Honk honk
honk
honk honk
h-h-h-honk!"

"Mi mi
mew mew
mew."

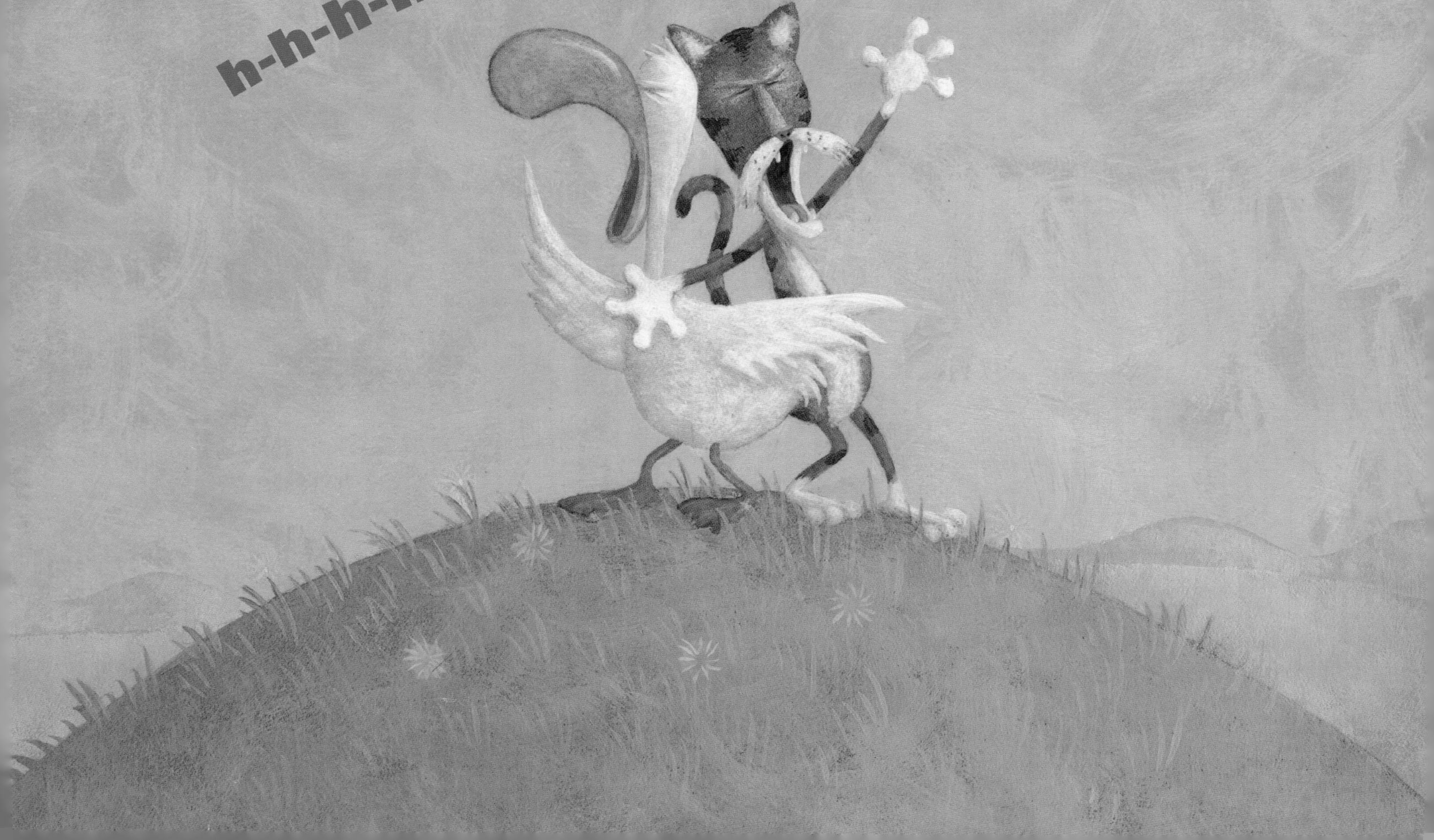

The hen bristled. "Ha! My cluck is *positively* operatic!

"Cluck cluck cluck cluck. Cluck cluck. P'awk! P'awk! P'awk!"

The pig interrupted the squawking soprano. "It is not crowing but crooning that is needed here. I am the proper baritone to complement that cow."

"YOU?"

"Me," said the pig. "Listen and observe: **Oink oink oink oink!**"

"Ha! **P'awk cluck cluck cluck!**"

"**Oink oink oink—snort!**"

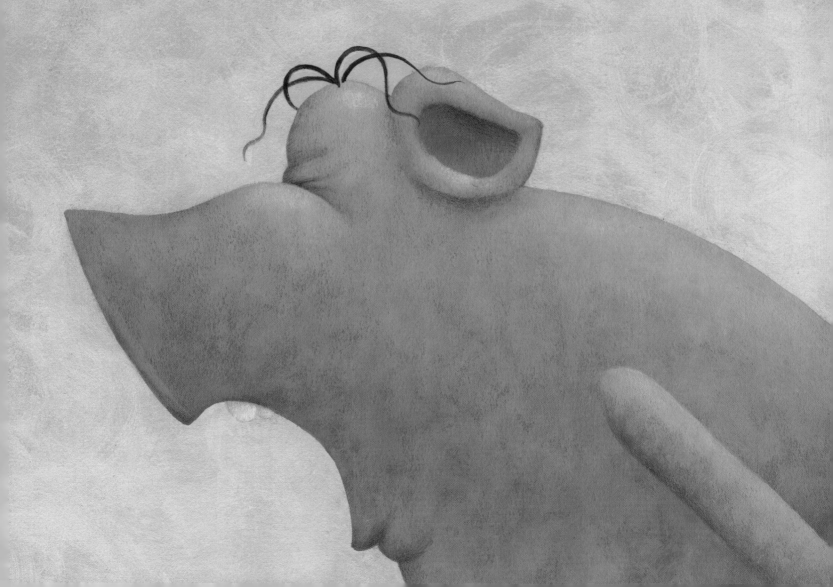

"Hold it down! Zip it! Quiet!" shouted the goose.
The four stared at one another. Then the goose giggled.
"You know something . . . that wasn't half bad. In fact, it sounded
pretty good! Let's try that again." He tapped his foot on a downbeat.
"And a one—and a two—"

"Honk honk honk cluck cluck snort me-ooooooow!"

The pig blushed with excitement. "Oh, my dears, we should form a chorus and sing along with Hilda!"

"But we need more singers for a whole chorus," advised the cat.

Many more singers, they all agreed.

Auditions began that very afternoon.
There was quite a turnout. . . .

"Baaa-baaa-b-a-a-

"Doodle-doodle-**doo!**"

"Woof. Woof. **Woof. Woof! Arf!** Arf! Bow-wow!"

"Ribbit."

That will wake them up!

You nailed it, dog!

If I had a shoe, I'd throw it.

Next!

"Nay! Nay! Nay! Nay! Nay! Nay-nay-nay nay-nay **nay!**"

"**. . . Quack!**"

"Squeak squeak **squeak squeak squeak!**"

You nailed it, rodent!

Strong, yet so sensitive.

Completely one-note. You're as flat as your feet!

Next!

And just when they had heard all there was
to hear—the cows came home.

"Moooo-moooo-moo!"

"Moo-moo-moo-mooooo!"

"NAY! NAY!"

"Squeak!"

"Baa!"

"Woof! Arf!"

"Ribbit!"

It was quite a chorus. The four were certain no one would be able to hear a wayward mi-mi-moo from *Hilda* even if they tried.

They all applauded.

"Fabulous! Superb! We love it!"

The question was . . . would Miss Heifer? And would she tra-la-la along with them?

The sun was setting just as Hilda bounded across the meadow. The barnyard chorus was so excited they burst into song to greet her.

"Mew!"

"Baa-aaa-aaaa-aaaa!"

"Honk!"

"Nay!"

"Doodle-doodle-doo."

"Bow-wow-oh-wow!"

"Ribbit!"

"Squeak!"

"Oink!"

"Squawk! P'awk!"

"Moo-moo-moo."

Hilda was baffled. Bewildered. Completely befuddled.

"HuuuUUH?"

"You ain't heard nothin' yet!" honked the goose.

"Surprise!" sang out the cat.
"We formed a chorus so you could sing
along with friends. Now you won't be sad or
lonely, and your moo will never be blue again!"

Hilda grinned. "Me? Mi-Mi-MOO with all of yooooooooou?
How too-toooo grand. But . . . I've given up singing."

"What?"

"To be honest," said Hilda, "I don't think I can really sing."
The pig raised his eyebrows. *"No kidding."*
Hilda nodded. "Yup. I'm giving it up."
The pig immediately removed his earplugs and smiled broadly.
"Bravo! A gloriously intelligent decision, my dear!"

The cow grinned. "It's true. I am definitely not a singer. I have the soul of a *dancer*! I'm a heifer who's a hoofer! Who knew I was so light on my feet!"

Thump

Thump

Thumpa-thumpa

Boom!

"Quick!

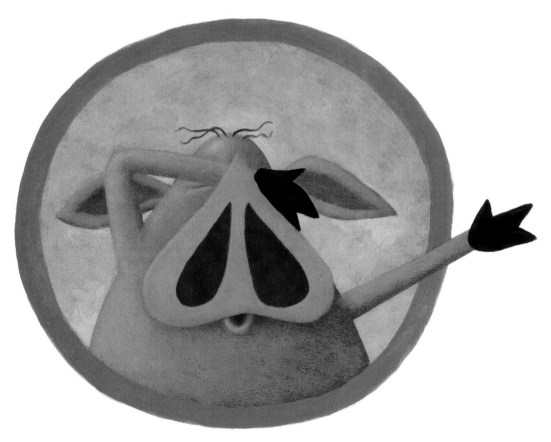

Somebody hand me my ice pack."